Puffin Books

The Village Dinosaur

The men at the quarry find something extraordinary in the pit, and haul it out with their cranes. Jed Watkins runs to see with all the rest of the village, and there before his eyes is the largest and strangest-looking creature he has ever seen!

'It's a dinosaur!' he yells. He's never been so thrilled in his life, but the Parish Clerk turns pale and says they will have to get rid of it. It tramples on fences and eats his vegetable marrows, and knocks down the village inn. On the other hand, it puts the village on the map in more ways than one, discovering an underground river and stopping a train crash, so that even the Parish Clerk thinks he might be worth all the trouble – that is, until Dino makes his last discovery of all!

Phyllis Arkle was born and educated in Chester, but has now lived for some years in Berkshire. She is actively interested in village life and in the Women's Institute movement. She enjoys reading, music and the countryside.

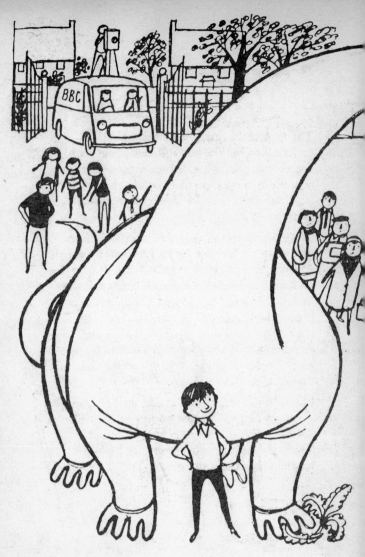

Other books by Phyllis Arkle

PHYLLIS ARKLE

The Village Dinosaur

Illustrated by Eccles Williams

PUFFIN BOOKS

PUFFIN BOOKS

Published by the Penguin Group
27 Wrights Lane, London W8 5TZ, England
Viking Penguin Inc., 40 West 23rd Street, New York, New York 10010, USA
Penguin Books Australia Ltd, Ringwood, Victoria, Australia
Penguin Books Canada Ltd, 2801 John Street, Markham, Ontario, Canada L3R 1B4
Penguin Books (NZ) Ltd, 182–190 Wairau Road, Auckland 10, New Zealand

Penguin Books Ltd, Registered Offices: Harmondsworth, Middlesex, England

First published by Brockhampton Press
(now Hodder & Stoughton Children's Books Ltd) 1968
Published in Puffin Books 1979
20 19 18 17 16 15

Set, printed and bound in Great Britain by
Cox & Wyman Ltd, Reading
Set in Monotype Plantin

Contents

1. Discovery in a chalk-pit

'What's going on?'
  'Something exciting!'
  'Where?'
  'Down at the old quarry.'
The news flashed through the village and shopkeepers locked up their shops and ran. Housewives rushed out of their houses without even bothering to bolt the doors.

Jed Watkins raced along – as usual, well behind the other boys – down the narrow, muddy, rutted lane leading to the disused chalk-pit. He could smell wood burning. Whatever could have happened? It was at a time like this that he wished he wasn't so much smaller than other boys of his age. He couldn't run as fast and he was always last on the scene.

When, panting, he arrived at the pit, most of the villagers were already there and two cranes were parked nearby. The crowd had made a ring round a bonfire, which shot up sparks, golden against the towering white chalk cliffs. People at the back stood on their toes and stretched their necks to see over or between the heads of those in front.

When he jumped up as high as he could, Jed glimpsed something lying beside the bonfire, something large and mound-like. He ran round trying to find a niche through which he could squeeze his way to the front, but no one would give way an inch. So he tried to make sense out of all the talking and shouting.

A workman from an adjacent building site raised his voice. 'Yes, yes, I'm telling you. I drove into the quarry to pick up some rubble and before you could say "Jack Robinson" the ground gave way. My mate and I managed to jump clear and the lorry disappeared into that large hole over there.'

In a voice trembling with excitement, the other man took up the tale. 'So we brought the crane and hoisted the lorry up. And it was then we noticed something large and round deep, deep down at the bottom. We lowered ourselves into the hole – we didn't like it a bit, I can tell you – and with our pickaxes we carefully prised it out of a layer of fine red sandstone, just below the chalk level. Then we had to send for another crane, as one wasn't strong enough to haul up this gigantic specimen. We put slings round his body and hooked them on to the cranes.

'And here he is safe and sound on firm ground. Looks to me as though he might revive when he's warmed up.'

Jed couldn't stand it any longer. Getting down on all fours and unheeding the protests of a woman who whacked him with her umbrella, and another who trod on his fingers, he pushed his way through the forest of legs. And there, lying beside the bonfire, was the largest and strangest-looking creature Jed had ever seen.

The beast stirred and Jed, watching wide-eyed, shouted, 'Look! He's waking up.'

The animal slowly lifted up its small head

supported on its long neck. Jed could see that a great part of the length of the animal was made up by the very long neck and the very long tapering tail, with a big body in the middle. He let out a whoop.

'It's a dinosaur! It's a dinosaur!' he yelled, throwing out his arms and jumping up and down.

The Parish Clerk, who was standing next to Jed, went pale. 'Don't be so ridiculous, Jed,' he chided. 'There haven't been any dinosaurs on this planet for millions and millions and millions of years.'

But Mr Holloway, Jed's headmaster, had managed to make his way through the crowd. 'Just a minute,' he said, examining the creature. 'Jed's right!' he said excitedly. 'It *is* a dinosaur! He must have been preserved all this time. He probably got wedged between two rocks and was buried by a sudden sandstorm. There must have been a crack in the layers of rock which have formed on top of him and air has filtered through. All very mysterious, I must say. I've heard of toads and birds – swifts and swallows, and an occasional nightjar – hiber-

nating, but this beats all! We might find an explanation one day.' He took a closer look. 'He's a young dinosaur by the size of him.'

'But he's *huge*, sir, really immense. Much, much bigger than an elephant, and just look at his long, long tail and neck,' Jed cried.

'Well he could grow twice as large – up to 80 feet or so long.'

'Phew!' said Jed. 'We'll call him "Dino", shall we?' In his own mind Jed had already adopted the creature.

'That sounds a bit obvious, doesn't it?' laughed Mr Holloway. 'But it will do for the time being. Yes, let's call him "Dino".'

'But what on earth are we going to do with him?' asked the Parish Clerk, who was beginning to feel somehow responsible for the strange new member of the community. The crowds pressed back as Dino slowly heaved up his enormous bulk and stood on all fours, his head on its long neck stretching far above the heads of the people. Jed stood his ground and Mr Holloway said reassuringly, 'It's all right. He can't bite much with those weak-looking teeth. Just watch out for his tail. He could lash out with that if he felt like it, but I'm sure he's quite docile. He's probably far more wary of us than we are of him.'

So Jed put out a trembling hand and actually touched the small horny scales on Dino's right front leg, noticing as he did so that Dino's front legs were shorter than his hind legs – and they were all slightly bandy! Jed's father, Mr Watkins, who stood not far away, looked admiringly at his small son standing beside the great beast.

'Jed always did have a way with animals,' he said. And Jed had never felt so pleased and proud. For the first time in his life he didn't mind being small.

'Could I have Dino as a pet?' he asked.

The crowd roared, and Mr Watkins joked, 'I'd rather like to see him sitting beside our living-room fire. There'd only be room for his head. And what a head!'

Jed looked up at Dino who was certainly no beauty. In fact, one might say that his rather snake-like head was distinctly ugly. His nose and eyes were on top of his head and his mouth stretched the length of his jaws. But Jed thought he was wonderful.

As warmth seeped through his bones, Dino shook himself and moved his long tail to and fro. The villagers hastily drew back out of reach of Dino's tail, but they shouted encouragingly at him.

Jed called out louder than anyone, 'Come on, Dino. Come on. See if you can walk.'

The Parish Clerk held up his hand. 'We must be practical,' he announced solemnly. 'Dino has been discovered in our village. Yes, well, all right, within the village boundary – well, *underneath* to be precise – and we'll have to do something about him. Has anybody got any ideas?'

'Could he live on the school playing-field, sir?' suggested Jed, who thought he would be able to keep an eye on Dino there.

But Mr Holloway wouldn't hear of it.

'No, no, no. It takes me all my time keeping you boys interested in your lessons without the added distraction of a dinosaur in the playground.'

'Well, what about the recreation ground? That's large enough, surely.' The Parish Clerk sounded impatient.

Jed's spirits rose, for Mr Watkins was warden of the recreation ground and Jed lived with his father and mother in a cottage on the grounds, near to the new village hall. Dino would live almost in Jed's own back garden. He could hardly wait for his father's reply.

After giving the matter some thought, Mr Watkins replied, 'That's the best idea so far. Dino can sleep alongside the hall. He'll be sheltered there and we'll have to see about getting a load of straw to make a bed for him.'

'What about food?' inquired the Parish Clerk. 'The village certainly can't afford to keep him. Everybody is still grumbling about the cost of the new hall, let alone having a dinosaur to look after.'

Much to Jed's relief, Mr Holloway was

ready with an answer. 'Dino won't need a tremendous amount of food. He's a plant-eater, not a savage carnivore, so perhaps the farmers would provide a few cabbages and leeks, and other vegetables, to be going on with. The boys can go round collecting leaves and wild plants. We'll have to find out what really suits him.'

'Well, for goodness' sake, let's get him to the recreation ground for a start,' suggested the Parish Clerk. 'We can't stand about here all day. I've got work to do if no one else has.' He waved his arms and clucked at Dino, trying to shoo him down the lane towards the village, but the animal appeared quite unconcerned and waited patiently.

Mr Holloway explained. 'Dino has got such a small brain, it probably takes some time for an idea to penetrate.' He tried giving the animal a light tap on the shoulder with a branch he had picked up off the ground, but all to no avail.

So Jed thought he'd try. Walking away directly in front of Dino, he called over his shoulder, 'Good fellow, Dino, come on, follow me!' and whether it was because Jed had a soft, pleasant, persuasive voice, or whether Dino had, from the first, taken a liking to the boy no one ever knew but, to everyone's amazement, Dino started to move slowly and ponderously down the lane, his large feet making deep holes in the mud.

The Parish Clerk, Mr Holloway and Mr Watkins followed some way behind as they thought it was wise to keep well clear of Dino's long tail. After them came men, women and children with a few dogs joining in to add to the confusion. It was quite a festive occasion and only lacked the village band to make it as good as the Bank Holiday procession.

As they passed through the village Dino occasionally swished his tail and turned his head from side to side. He walked bang in the middle of the road. Oncoming traffic had to pull in to one side, and lorries and cars, hooting impatiently, queued behind. And the astonishment on the faces of the motorists!

17

Never before had they seen anyone so small as Jed leading anything as large as Dino. In fact, never before had they encountered anything remotely resembling Dino.

The local woman reporter, who represented a newspaper in a nearby town, happened to be in the village. She whipped a notebook and pencil out of her pocket and, joined by the local photographer, followed the procession.

2. Dino settles down

Jed turned down the lane leading to the recreation ground and opened wide the double gates at the end.

'Come on, Dino,' he urged. 'You'll just about manage to squeeze through.' But Dino, who, to give him his due, had never seen a gate before, stepped aside and put first one large strong-clawed foot and then another on top of the fence, crushing it like matchwood. The Parish Clerk wrung his hands.

'Oh, dear me, dear me, what *are* we going to do? Dino will ruin us. We'll have to get rid of him somehow!'

'Don't worry, sir. I'll mend the fence,' called out Mr Watkins quickly.

Dino obviously recognized shelter when he saw it, for he headed straight for the double glass doors leading into the village hall. He was very surprised when the glass splintered all over his head.

Jed cried out in alarm, 'Oh, oh, he'll hurt himself. Come out, Dino.'

'He'll be all right,' said Mr Holloway. 'His hide is thicker than an elephant's.'

And sure enough, Dino, looking bewildered, shook the glass from his head like drops of water. He again tried to push his way into the hall, but his neck stuck half-way, so, backing clear, he allowed Jed to lead him to the side of the building.

The Parish Clerk clutched his head in his hands and moaned, 'Just look at those plate-glass doors. It will take a lot of ratepayers' money to replace them. Whatever are we going to do?'

Meanwhile, the reporter had been asking questions of everybody and the photographer rushed about viewing Dino from all angles.

Jed's schoolfellows formed an admiring group round Dino, but Mr Holloway called them away.

'Not too many at a time. We don't want to frighten Dino.'

Jed had his photograph taken while standing underneath Dino's neck in front of his legs. There was plenty of room and he wasn't in the least afraid.

When he had run out of film the photographer, with the reporter, rushed off down the lane. The reporter called out. 'My word! What a scoop. First in the field all right this time. My editor will be pleased. You'd better look out – all the others will be here soon.' She was right. By the time Dino had settled down and had been fussed over by everybody, the 'others' arrived. There was a screeching of brakes.

'Look! Here come the television men,' shouted the boys, running to meet the two teams who were soon busily unloading equipment and setting it up near Dino's corner. From then on everything was in a state of turmoil. Each team tried to get into the best position for filming Dino, while still more reporters and also many curious sight-seers added to the confusion. The centre of all the attraction took little notice of what was going on around him. Squatting on his haunches, he continued sampling the different kinds of vegetables and plants which were offered to him.

Men shouted, pushed and directed and ran about everywhere, over the football pitch and the tennis-courts. One man fell into the paddling pool. The recreation ground, slightly squelchy from recent rain, became a quagmire. No one took any notice of the Parish Clerk who, poor man, was walking round in utter despair.

'We'll never, never, balance the accounts this year after we've repaired all this damage. We'll be ruined, absolutely ruined,' he cried to no one in particular, raising his arms skywards. But the excitement and all the hurry and bustle went on around him, and it was getting dark when the filming ceased and the cameramen and reporters dashed back to London. The sightseers then thought about supper and departed with many a backward glance at Dino.

The boys were reluctant to leave and stayed near to Dino with Mr Holloway and Jed's father. The Parish Clerk surveyed the havoc. He shook his clenched fist at a lone cameraman, struggling back to his van.

'How dare you come here without permission ... and ... and ... spoil our ground! Just look at it. Who's going to pay for the repairs, I ask you? Did you think of that?' he shrieked, outraged.

The man looked surprised. 'Calm down, guv,' he replied. 'No one has ever seen a dinosaur before. He'll be a gold-mine if you handle him properly. But you'll have a job keeping him, I can tell you. Everybody will be after him. He'll be on the front pages of all the newspapers and on the television screens

too. The film companies will be after him
next. There's a fortune to be made out of that
animal. He'll be the sensation of the cen-
tury!'

'*Will* he?' The Parish Clerk looked more
kindly at Dino. 'Now, I wonder . . . ? Jed, give
Dino some more food and perhaps he'd prefer
milk to drink.' He turned to one of the other
boys. 'Go and see if your father can spare
a gallon or two. Tell him we'll pay later.'

The Parish Clerk hadn't finished. He
paced about and then spread out his arms
wide. 'I think we'll have to consider building
a shelter for Dino here, alongside the hall
where there are no windows.'

'Can we afford it?' asked Mr Holloway.

The Parish Clerk ignored the interruption.

By now, the other boys had been sent off
home. Jed wanted to stay with Dino, but his
father said, 'No, that won't be necessary.
He'll be all right.'

Mr Holloway added, 'I expect Dino will
want to have a good nap – when he's decided
he's had enough to eat, that is.'

'We couldn't exactly *lose* him, could we?'
remarked the Parish Clerk happily.

So Jed went home. His mother had cooked
an excellent hot-pot to warm them up, but
Jed wasn't hungry. He could talk of nothing
else but Dino, until his mother, exasperated,
said,

'Now, Jed, up to bed you go, otherwise
you'll not be fit for school in the morning.

Mind you, I don't think any of us will be good for much tomorrow after today's events! Oh, all right, you can have just one last look at Dino. Put your wellingtons on.'

Jed went outside and gazed up at the few clouds scudding across an otherwise starry, moonlit sky and looked around at the lighted windows in the houses bordering the ground. He plodded through the mud, enjoying the sucking and plopping noises of each dragging step. As he approached Dino, he saw that the great beast was resting with his head and tail curled round towards his body. Dino raised his head, snuffled a little, and went to sleep again. He didn't object when Jed gave him an approving pat on the top of his head.

Satisfied, and with a warm glow in his heart, Jed made his way back to the cottage and climbed wearily up the stairs. He thought about Dino before he went to sleep and he dreamed about him when he was asleep. In the middle of the night he woke with a start and leapt out of bed and crossed over to the window. He could see the huge elephant-like body of Dino, bathed in moonlight, safe and sound.

It was daylight when Jed woke up again. Jumping out of bed he dashed across to the window. He couldn't believe his eyes. Dino had vanished! Opening the window he peered round, but there was no sign of the animal.

'He's gone! He's disappeared!' wailed Jed, running across the landing into his parents' bedroom.

'Who's gone?' asked Mr Watkins sleepily.

'Dino's not in his corner. I can't see him anywhere.'

His father got out of bed. 'Get your clothes on,' he said urgently. 'We'll go and search. He can't have gone very far.'

'Oh, dear me,' sighed Mrs Watkins, yawning. 'Dino's going to be more trouble than a cartload of monkeys.'

Jed and his father searched everywhere they could think of and then Mr Watkins sent Jed off to alert Mr Holloway and the

Parish Clerk, who very soon joined them in
the silent, deserted street.

'He must be somewhere near,' said Mr
Holloway. 'It's extremely unlikely that he's
travelled very far – he moves so slowly. But
I'll get out my car and we'll scout around the
countryside. You'd better come with me,
Jed.'

So Jed and Mr Holloway got into the car
and drove over the river bridge and along the
country lanes, keeping a sharp look-out in all
directions for a small head on top of a long
neck but without success. They returned to
the village.

The Parish Clerk was very upset. 'Oh,
what on earth can we do?' he cried. 'We just
can't afford to lose Dino. He's going to be
such an asset to this village. You don't think
he's been stolen, do you?'

'No, I don't,' replied Mr Holloway shortly.
'And don't forget that yesterday you were
wanting to get rid of him.'

'Yes, yes, I know, but it's different now.'

Suddenly Mr Holloway snapped his

fingers. 'Did you look in the river?' he asked Jed.

'I searched along the meadows,' answered Jed, puzzled.

'No, no, did you look *in* the river?'

'Well, no.'

'Oh, for pity's sake, don't say he's been drowned,' shouted the Parish Clerk. 'Come on, let's go,' and they raced through the street again, over the bridge and down on to the river bank. Now, it was only a small river, being a tributary of a much larger river, but it was quite deep in the centre. The surface, rippled by a gentle breeze, glistened in the rays of the early morning sun, and a few swans and ducks could be seen in the distance by the old mill. Suddenly Jed pointed upstream.

'What's that?' he cried.

'It's Dino,' said Mr Holloway.

'Where?' asked the Parish Clerk and Mr Watkins.

'Over there,' and Mr Holloway pointed out two small ears, two eyes and a nose sticking up out of the water. The eyes had evidently observed Jed, for Dino got up slowly and waded into shallow water. The swans and ducks bounced about on the waves. Jed and his friends all ran to meet him.

'Is he all right?' asked the Parish Clerk anxiously.

'Of course he is,' replied Mr Holloway impatiently. 'Haven't you noticed that his nostrils are placed with his eyes on top of his head? He can breathe and see even though almost completely under the water. That was how dinosaurs used to hide from their enemies.' The Parish Clerk was too relieved to bother about Dino's anatomy, and still more relieved when Dino obediently followed Jed back to the recreation ground.

3. Dino goes for a walk

Dino settled down in his corner contentedly enough and as he had his head well down, Jed was able to talk right into his ear. 'I want you to understand that you're quite safe here with us, Dino. We're going to look after you and there's no need to hide away. You've no enemies.'

'No natural enemies,' agreed Mr Holloway, who had overheard, 'but if I'm not mistaken there's more trouble approaching. Come on, Jed, the school bell has rung. We'll have to leave the Parish Clerk and your father to deal with matters. Oh, I realize we haven't had any breakfast,' he added, 'but we'll have to do without food until lunch-time. You can't expect to lead a normal life when you have a dinosaur on your hands!'

Jed, following Mr Holloway, glanced apprehensively at the two men they passed in the lane, and the Parish Clerk and Mr Watkins greeted the men, both tall and neat and dressed in city-clothes. They were from the Ministry of Health and were very curious about Dino. They started asking questions immediately.

'Quarantine?' repeated the Parish Clerk incredulously. 'Put Dino into quarantine? Whatever for?'

'The public has to be protected, and all animals arriving in this country have to go into quarantine for six months,' one man explained. 'Dino might have cholera, plague or even yellow fever.'

'Nonsense!' exploded the Parish Clerk. 'And in any case, he hasn't "arrived in this country". He's been here all along. Much longer than any of us.' (The Parish Clerk laughed at his own joke.) 'He's perfectly healthy. Take a look at him.'

The advice was unnecessary, for the men couldn't keep their eyes off Dino. 'Oh, I

33

grant you he *appears* to be in good condition, but you can't go by that. He'll have to be examined by our vet.'

'He's staying right here,' replied the Parish Clerk, with a 'you-try-and-take-him-away' expression on his face. The two men looked uncertain, and then one of them thought of something. 'Well, then, may we inspect your licence?' he asked triumphantly.

The Parish Clerk was very indignant. 'Where do I get a dinosaur licence? Tell me that. Do I have to go to Whitehall for one?' he asked sarcastically.

The men could tell they were making no headway so, with a last look at Dino, they left. 'All right. We'll have to see what the Minister of Health has to say about this. You'll be hearing from us,' was their parting shot.

The Parish Clerk was fuming. 'Think they can take Dino away from us, do they? Well, they can think again. Come on, Mr Watkins, we'd better go and see about those estimates.'

Dino watched them out of sight and munched and chewed his food all morning. Then, standing up, he peered over the roof of the hall towards the school. Head on one side, his sharp eyes scanned the landscape. Then he ambled down the lane, this time putting all four feet on top of another section of fencing.

He didn't hurry. There were many interesting things for him to inspect. For instance, at one point over the hedge he saw a row of marrows. He didn't, of course, know they were marrows. To him, they were just delicious-looking morsels. He craned his long neck over the tall hedge and worked his way through the row by taking a bite out of each vegetable.

Just then the Parish Clerk and Mr Watkins came back, closely followed by Jed, out of school now because it was lunch time. The Parish Clerk let out an agonized yell. 'Just look at him now! Come away, you great beast! He's eaten all the marrows I was growing for the Horticultural Show. There's

35

not a perfect one left. Oh, oh, I can't stand any more of this. He'll have to go. I've made up my mind.'

Jed and Mr Watkins stood helplessly while Dino, alarmed by the Parish Clerk waving his hat at him, set off at a slightly smarter pace towards the village.

'Stop him, Jed! Stop him! Heaven only knows what mischief he'll get up to next,' cried the Parish Clerk.

'I'll try, sir,' panted Jed, running on ahead. But Dino was evidently enjoying himself and he didn't halt until he reached the ancient inn at the village cross-roads. He could just about see over the rooftop of the two-storeyed inn and gazed at the green fields and, beyond, the river running like a silver thread through the meadows.

The Parish Clerk, breathless, red in the face and with his hat on the back of his head, came up wielding a spanner he had borrowed from the garage farther down the road.

'Oh, don't hit him, please, sir,' pleaded Jed.

'Don't worry. It would take more than a

blow from this spanner to do much harm, but we've got to turn him back somehow,' answered the Parish Clerk, striking Dino smartly across the tail.

But he was mistaken, for Dino moved more quickly than anyone thought possible. As he swung round, his enormous tail lashed against the side wall of the inn. There was a noise like thunder as the bricks and mortar came toppling down. It was just as though a heavy lorry had crashed into the inn and razed one end of it to the ground. The innkeeper and his wife came rushing out into the street and everyone jumped back choking and spluttering. Dino had backed down the road away from the inn. It was not until the dust had cleared a little that they could see exactly what had happened.

'Thousands . . .' muttered the Parish Clerk, his eyes glazed.

'Thousands of what, sir?' asked Jed, anxious to take the Clerk's mind off things.

'Thousands and thousands and thousands of pounds it will cost us before that beast has

finished. This settles it. The Ministry of Health can have him – and welcome. I'll inform them straight away. My nerves won't stand any more.'

'What's going on?' asked Mr Holloway, who had just arrived.

Jed replied tearfully. 'Oh, sir, the Parish Clerk hit Dino across his tail and he swerved right round. He shouldn't be frightened like that.'

'Hm, hm, that's interesting,' said Mr Holloway. 'I imagine it is because Dino has got a sort of nerve centre, which is very important to him, at the base of his spine. It helps him to control his very heavy hind legs. We'll have to remember not to alarm him by touching him on the back, unless we really want him to move.'

'We won't want him to move,' said the Parish Clerk.

'And why not?'

'Because he won't be here. I'm going to
telephone the Ministry of Health. They can
come and fetch him. The sooner the better so
far as I'm concerned.'

There were murmurs from the crowd, and
even the innkeeper, surveying the damage,
shook his head in disapproval at the thought
of losing Dino. As to Jed, it was almost more
than he could bear. He didn't think he could
face anyone. Looking at the ground he idly
scuffed away at the dust and rubble with the
soles of his shoes. Suddenly, he bent down
and with his bare hands swept a little pile of
rubbish to one side.

'Mr Holloway, sir,' he called out, now on
his hands and knees. 'Come and look at this.'

Everybody crowded round and Dino
ambled forward, flicked his ears and lowered
his head as though he too was anxious to see
what Jed had unearthed.

Mr Holloway got out his handkerchief and
enthusiastically cleared away more rubble.
'I think you've made an important discovery,

Jed. I'm sure this is Roman tiling. Look, it's coloured marble, cut and arranged in a pattern. The inn obviously stands on the site of a Roman villa.'

He called to the Parish Clerk, who was on his way to the telephone. 'It's worth your while coming back to see what I've found.'

The Clerk turned back reluctantly. 'Well, what is it? A few golden sovereigns?' he asked churlishly. 'It will cost more than that to repair the damage caused by this dinosaur.'

'Much more valuable than a few sovereigns. There are the foundations of a Roman house under this inn, which means there must have been a settlement here. Many people will be interested in this discovery. Good old Dino!'

Jed scrubbed away. 'Look, sir, here's a piece,' he said, pointing at a portion of red marble now clearly visible.

'Looks like a very ordinary bit of tiling to me,' muttered the Parish Clerk uncertainly.

'Oh, no, it isn't,' said the headmaster. 'It's

similar to the floors found at the Roman fort further up the river. Dino's stirring things up in this village. And not before time, I might add.'

'Can he stay, then, please?' asked Jed quickly.

'Well, er . . . for the time being, anyway,' agreed the Clerk. 'After all, we can do with more visitors coming to the village. That's always good for trade. Yes, yes, of course he must stay. Just let anyone try taking him away. I'll be ready for them.'

Mr Holloway grinned at Jed.

The Parish Clerk turned to the local saddler, whose shop stood opposite the old inn. 'That animal is going to do a lot of good for this village,' he announced. 'As a matter of interest, I wonder how many hands he is?'

'He's not a horse!' cried the saddler. However, starting at the tip of Dino's tail, he paced slowly along until he came to the animal's oustretched head.

'At a rough guess, I should say he's getting

on for 40 feet long, and you can see for your-
self how tall he is.'

'And he's growing!' groaned the Parish
Clerk.

Dino seemed to be getting his bearings, for
he turned round, carefully avoiding scrap-
ing the buildings with his tail. Then he
slowly made his way back to the recreation
ground.

And there was peace and quietness in the
village for a time.

4. Dino raises the alarm

Jed had gone on ahead, and before going back to school, made sure there was a fresh supply of vegetables for Dino. The dinosaur was no trouble at all for the rest of that day. He slept most of the time and ate unhurriedly for almost all the rest of the time. This seemed to be his idea of contentment.

After school, Jed's first thought was of Dino and, joined by several friends, he ran across to the recreation ground. There was a stranger with Dino – a big fat man who puffed away at a cigar. As the boys came running up, he said,

'My, my, you've got an enormous pet here, haven't you? I'd like to speak to someone about this animal. Who's in charge?' One of the boys went off to fetch the Parish Clerk.

'Good afternoon. What can I do for you?' asked the Clerk politely when he arrived.

'I've come on behalf of the Zoological Society,' explained the man. 'My committee wish to make an offer for Dino.'

'But he's not for sale,' replied the Clerk. 'We've no intention of selling him. He's the most valuable thing this village has ever possessed.'

The man persisted. 'Come now, we're much better suited to keep a dinosaur. After all, in a way he's related to the crocodiles and we've several of those reptiles in our zoo. And we've made a special study of diet and ventilation – all that sort of thing. He'll be much better off in captivity.'

'Oh, no, he won't,' shouted the Parish Clerk. 'There's nothing Dino likes better than a stroll now and then.' (He didn't think it necessary to enlarge on what had taken place on these excursions.) 'And we'd all hate to see him in an enclosure.'

The boys added their views.

'Dino will be happy in the village. The

Parish Clerk is having a shelter built for him here, alongside the hall.'

'And lots of people will be coming to see Dino and examine the Roman remains underneath the inn.'

'He's better than a gold-mine.'

But the man was determined not to give up easily. 'We'll pay you five hundred pounds for him,' he said.

'We wouldn't accept five thousand pounds, thank you,' replied the Parish Clerk, with just the faintest suggestion of weakening in his voice. 'And it's no use trying to bargain with us. We've quite made up our minds.'

The man had one last try. 'Six thousand pounds,' he offered.

After a split second's hesitation, the Parish Clerk bellowed, 'No, no, no. We're keeping him for good.'

The man shrugged his shoulders. 'Well, I hope you won't regret it, that's all I can say. Here's my card in case you should change your mind.' He departed.

Dino lowered his head to take another mouthful of cabbage and Jed whispered, 'Did you hear? It's all right. No one's going to take you away. The Parish Clerk just said that he's made up his mind you're going to stay with us always.'

Jed waited until the Parish Clerk and the boys had left before he too went home for supper.

In the middle of the night Dino woke up. The sky was clear and bright and there was a full moon. He probably felt restless. Perhaps he was remembering the Age of Reptiles long ago when, with his fellow dinosaurs, he walked through the swamps and forests. Then, there were no creatures mightier than the dinosaurs.

Dino went down to the river, waded through it and wandered over the cultivated fields on the other side. What a glorious supply of food stretched in orderly rows in front of him. There were hundreds and hundreds of curly kale. He plodded along eating while in his wake appeared deep dinosaur footprints and mangled vegetables.

When he had had his fill, he set off slowly towards the village. He was getting quite good at judging when it was possible to squeeze his huge bulk down a narrow street and he eased his tail gently round corners without knocking into anything. As he moved sedately along the main street, he inspected the shops and houses on each side. It was a warm night and most of the bedroom windows were open. Dino peered into some as he passed. When he came to the Parish Clerk's house he stopped. Who knows? Perhaps he recognized the Clerk, sleeping peacefully in bed? Dino pushed his snout right through the window and gave a loud snort.

This woke up the Parish Clerk's wife, who was lying on the side of the bed nearer to the window. Seeing Dino's gleaming eyes – and being half asleep anyway – she let out a mighty shriek.

'Fire! Fire! Fire' she yelled, throwing off the bed-clothes and rushing to the door.

The Parish Clerk woke up with a start.

'Fire?' he shouted. 'Where?' and without waiting for an answer, he ran downstairs and dialled 'Emergency', shouting down the telephone, 'Fire! Parish Clerk's house,' before slamming down the receiver.

By the time he had pulled on an overcoat and followed his wife out into the street most

of the villagers had been awakened by the eerie sound of the siren splitting the silence. Heads popped out of windows and a few men rushed down into the street.

Jed was out of bed as soon as he heard the siren. He checked that Dino was not in his corner and then, throwing a coat over his shoulders and without waiting for permission, he ran off towards the village. He arrived just as the fire-brigade rolled up, but the sight of Dino unharmed was all that mattered to Jed.

The firemen jumped down from the engine and proceeded to unroll the hoses. The leader called out.

'Where's the fire?'

By this time the Parish Clerk was beginning to feel a little foolish. He began to think there must have been a misunderstanding.

'Well, where *is* the fire?' he shouted at his wife.

She hummed and hawed while the men got more impatient. At last she pointed at Dino.

'Dino?' asked the Clerk disbelievingly. 'What's he got to do with it?'

'I think he must have stuck his head through the window and . . . and . . . when I saw his eyes, I thought . . .'

The Parish Clerk couldn't believe his ears, 'Mean to tell me we've all been roused in the middle of the night by that animal? Well, this time it's just too much. He'll have to go to the zoo. I'll see about it in the morning. My mind's finally made up.'

'Not again!' protested Mr Holloway, who was leaning out of the bedroom window of the schoolhouse opposite. 'First Dino's going – then he's staying – then he's going – just like a see-saw.'

The Parish Clerk threw up his arms. 'Well, you tell me what we're to do with him. I'm tired of hearing how valuable he is. But is he worth it, I ask you? What's he going to get up to next? We'll all be nervous wrecks if we're not going to be able to sleep at night – it's bad enough during the daytime.'

The policeman had arrived on his bicycle.

'There are enough bogus fire-alarms without an animal joining in the mischief,' he said severely.

And the firemen, muttering angrily, were about to leave when Dino lifted up his head and sniffed the air.

Jed looked up at him. 'I'm sure Dino can smell something. Yes, yes, now I can smell burning!' he cried.

They all raised their heads and sniffed. Suddenly a figure could be seen rushing down the street towards them. It was Mr Watkins, out of breath and gasping. 'There's a fire in the village hall. Hearing the siren, I guessed the fire-brigade would be somewhere down here.'

The firemen leapt to their positions, but, unfortunately, they couldn't get past Dino, who nearly filled the width of the street. There was a great hullabaloo as they reversed the machine back the way they had come and took a detour through the narrow back streets. The crowd followed, led by the Parish Clerk and Mr Holloway.

Jed stayed behind with Dino and eventually persuaded him to move. It took them a long time to get home, but Jed didn't mind. He was getting used to the fact that Dino moved so slowly. He waited until the animal, taking advantage of his great height, selected an apple from the top of a tall tree, and again while he nibbled at the green hedges bordering the lane. When they finally arrived at the recreation ground, the fire was well under control.

'What happened?' asked Jed.

'We think the fire started in a waste paper basket,' explained his father. 'It must have been smouldering for a couple of hours or so before bursting into flames. If it hadn't been for Dino, the hall might have been destroyed. I don't think I would have awakened if I hadn't heard the siren.'

'Dino is a real treasure in more ways than one,' said the Parish Clerk approvingly.

'Oh, here we go again,' said Mr Holloway. 'I suppose we're keeping him now?'

'Of course he's staying with us,' said the Clerk. He glanced at Dino. 'Look at those water plants clinging to his hide. He's evidently been in the water again. Seems to like it. Do you think it would be a good idea to dig a pool for him?'

'Well, it will cost quite a bit, but if the

ratepayers are prepared to subsidize it, I don't see why not,' agreed Mr Holloway.

'He's worth his weight in gold to us, is Dino,' said the Clerk.

Jed went back to bed feeling more contented. It would certainly appear that Dino was going to be allowed to stay with them, but he wished the Parish Clerk wouldn't keep changing his mind. After all, Dino couldn't be expected to stay quietly in his corner, day and night, could he? A growing dinosaur needed exercise.

5. Dino puts his foot in it

While the villagers were getting used to having a dinosaur among them, Jed thought that only his father understood exactly how much Dino meant to him now. The Parish Clerk had been busy getting the estimates for the building of a shelter, and also for a pool. He was not at all worried about the cost.

'You'll see,' he would say cheerfully, 'before very long Dino will put this village on the map. We'll be famous.'

It was true that there was no lack of interest in Dino and in the old inn. Archaeologists had been busy carefully removing some of the tiles which Dino had exposed, and taking them away for examination to the museum in the nearby town. In fact, everybody seemed happy – not least Dino, who still spent his days chewing and sleeping and occasionally taking a stately saunter.

Jed had almost got over his fear that he would lose Dino, when one day another stranger appeared. Jed was feeding Dino at the time and the man, tall and thin, smartly dressed and with a shrewd face, stood a few paces away. He took a good look at Dino and Jed, who was always close to Dino when danger threatened. They made a strange couple – rather like a lion and a mouse together.

The man came up to Jed. 'Who owns this animal?' he asked.

'Why, we do, of course.'

'Who are "we"?'

'All of us, the Parish Clerk and the villagers and . . . and . . . me, sir.'

'Well, will you please go and tell the
Parish Clerk that I'd like a word with him?'

So Jed, with a worried frown on his face,
ran off to the village and soon returned
accompanied by the Clerk.

'Now what's all this?' asked the Clerk.
'Who owns Dino? Hasn't Jed told you? We
own him, of course, and, what's more, no
one's going to take him away.'

'Perhaps you'll listen to what I've got to
say first,' replied the man. 'I'm the director
of a film company and they would like to buy
this dinosaur. Never before in our wildest
dreams did we think we'd have the oppor-
tunity of owning a dinosaur.'

'True – you're not going to have the
chance. He's not for sale.' The Parish Clerk's
voice was firm.

'We'll give a good price for him,' said the
director.

'Not interested. In any case we've already been offered six thousand pounds for him.'

'Ten thousand pounds, then,' said the man quietly.

The Parish Clerk wavered, but then he noticed Jed's stricken face and being at heart a kindly man – and also an honest one – he said, 'Still not interested. He's not mine to sell. He belongs to the whole village and, perhaps, especially to Jed, here.' Jed straightened his back with pride and relief and gave Dino another cabbage.

The man knew he was defeated. 'All right. I can tell you're determined not to bargain with me, but would you consider loaning him to us for, say, a week or two? We could do some good filming in that time. And the boy could come along as well. We could use him in the crowd scenes.'

The Parish Clerk thought about this. 'We'll see,' he replied. 'I'll have to put the matter before my council, and Jed's father would have to give his consent. I'll let you know our decision if you care to get in touch with me again. But it couldn't be for some time yet, as Dino has got to become really acclimatized here first.'

'I'll certainly come over again,' said the man without hesitation.

When he had gone the Parish Clerk turned to Jed. 'You know, he's got a point,' he mused. 'To whom does Dino really belong? I trust we have the right to keep him.'

Jed fervently hoped so. He had thought everything was going to be quite all right, but the Parish Clerk's words had put fear back into his heart.

Dino was very good for a day or so. Now and then he wandered round the recreation ground watching the children at play. Sometimes he went as far as the gate and seemed to be watching for Jed coming down the lane. Soon he'll know exactly what time I'm due home, thought Jed happily. He's better than any dog!

But one day Dino went off to do some more exploring. It was lunch-time and the few people in the street stood to one side and smiled at Dino. He was doing no damage and they didn't attempt to stop him. He treated himself to a leaf from one tree and a soft apple or two from another and even helped himself to a cauliflower from the open stall outside the greengrocer's shop.

Leaving the village behind, he came across an open space where the foundations for twelve new houses on an estate were being laid. The builders, having finished their picnic lunch, were resting under a tree reading newspapers. They didn't glance up.

Dino plodded slowly across the foundations, until at one point the ground started to give way. As he moved forward, he sank down, deeper and deeper and deeper until his legs were completely submerged. Just then one of the men glanced up.

'Hey, look!' he yelled at the top of his voice, 'Dino's disappearing into the ground again!'

They all leaped up and ran across. Dino was by now up to the top of his back in rubble. Only his head and neck were showing. Poor Dino! He was quite incapable of climbing out of the hole.

'Get the cranes – and the slings,' ordered the foreman. 'Good heavens! Pulling Dino out of craters is becoming a habit. And just look at the mess.'

With a great deal of effort and many encouraging shouts they eased him out. The Parish Clerk came running up just as Dino surfaced. He was speechless with wrath and amazement until Jed and Mr Holloway and some of the boys came along, when he found his voice.

'Look at that damage!' he croaked.

Mr Holloway spoke up. 'I told you all along that there was a stream running under

this field. Many a time as a boy have I lain down, put my ear to the ground and listened to the water gurgling away. But no, oh, dear me, no, you wouldn't listen to me.'

The Parish Clerk ignored him. 'More expense. I don't know what we're going to do . . .' he groaned.

'"Dino will have to go,"' quoted the headmaster.

'Who said he'd have to go?' asked the Parish Clerk sharply.

'Oh, I thought *you* were going to say it

again,' replied Mr Holloway mildly, winking at Jed.

'If anyone tries to take Dino away from this village, they'll have to reckon with me,' said the Parish Clerk. 'But, really, I don't know whether he's going to be worth it.' Off he strode, shaking his head, to fetch the architect.

By the time he arrived back Dino was once more on firm ground. He shook his head in bewildered fashion and swished his tail rather menacingly.

The architect inspected the ruined foundations and turned to the Parish Clerk. 'Well, well, well. Dino has certainly done us a good turn,' he said. 'There is an underground stream below this field – '

('I told you so,' said Mr Holloway to the Parish Clerk.)

' – and if Dino hadn't gone through like this, the houses might have collapsed one day.'

'But surely you tested the ground first?' grumbled the Parish Clerk.

'Yes, yes, of course, but the usual borings couldn't have reached as far down as the stream. The houses might have been quite safe, but on the other hand they might not. It's just as well Dino has discovered the weakness. He's a great animal, that dinosaur.'

'I can see I'm going to have a stormy council meeting tonight,' said the Clerk, 'but I'm standing by Dino. He's worth every penny he costs us. I've been thinking, Jed, he hasn't got a proper drinking trough, has he? I'll order a stone horse-trough for him.'

'Excellent,' agreed Mr Holloway. 'To be paid for out of the rates?'

Dino had wandered off and Jed discovered him sitting on his haunches by the hole in the chalk-pit.

'Come on, Dino, time to go back,' he said. Dino, with a backward glance down the hole, moved away.

Jed made a fuss of him and, when the small snake-like head was on a level with his own, told him, 'You're going to have a stone drinking trough, just like the ones horses use. And the Parish Clerk is *quite certain* – well, I *think* he is, I *hope* he is – you're going to stay with us for ever and ever. You're such a clever animal!'

6. Dino gets on the line

Jed slept much better at night, now that he felt assured Dino was going to stay with them. One morning, however, he woke up and discovered that Dino was missing again. He wasn't unduly alarmed. And not until he had gone out and searched everywhere – not forgetting to look in the river this time – did he begin to panic. He ran along to the Parish Clerk's house and knocked on the door. The Clerk popped his head out of the bedroom window.

'Missing? Not again!' he sighed. 'Oh, that beast. Why ever did I say that we'd keep him? There's no peace now. Ah, well, wait there, Jed. I'll be down soon.'

As he stepped into the street, the postman came along and, with a cheery, 'Good morning,' handed the Parish Clerk a bundle of letters.

'Have you seen Dino anywhere?' asked the Clerk. 'No? Well, we'll have to go and search, I suppose. No time for these now,' and he went back into the house and put the bundle of letters on the hall table. As he was turning away, he picked up one of the letters. 'Half a minute, Jed. This one looks important,' he said.

Opening the letter, he read it and then called out excitedly, 'Why, Jed, this is from the Minister of Health. He advises me that, after consultation, the government has decided that Dino belongs to us. He will be our sole responsibility. Come on, Jed, we've got to find that animal. Go and tell Mr Holloway he's missing again.'

In spite of his anxiety, Jed heaved a huge sigh of relief as he hurried across the road to the schoolhouse and roused Mr Holloway, who soon joined them.

'But you *can't* have looked everywhere,' he said. 'Not in the river? Nor by the hole in the old quarry? Dino has a habit lately of sitting there.'

Mr Holloway thought for a few minutes and then cried, 'Dash it all. Why didn't I think of it before? Remember the circus which passed through the village yesterday? I'll wager anything they've enticed Dino away. Come on, we'll get the car and go after him.'

Fortunately it was a Saturday, so there was no school to worry about. They climbed into the car and it seemed ages before they neared the outskirts of the town. They could see in the distance the flag on the big top. Jed, sitting tense on the back seat, leaned forward and peered between the heads of the Parish Clerk and Mr Holloway.

Then, 'There he is, there he is, over there!' he shouted, quite unnecessarily for both Mr Holloway and the Parish Clerk had caught a glimpse of the unmistakable small head at the end of the long neck. Mr Holloway stepped on the accelerator. As they passed through the gates into the field they could hear the roaring of lions and the chattering of monkeys and noises from other animals coming from the direction of the menagerie.

They parked the car and rushed off towards Dino who, as usual, was surrounded by an admiring though somewhat awe-struck group. Dino lowered his head, as he often did now when Jed approached, and Jed, his heart nearly bursting, gently pulled at his ears. He couldn't imagine how he could ever live without Dino now.

The Parish Clerk sent someone off to find the proprietor, who soon came bustling through the noisy crowd. When he could make himself heard, he was most apologetic.

'Yes, I'm really sorry about this. You see, two of my men spotted Dino as we passed through your village yesterday and, without a word to me, they went over last night and brought him here. Took them a long time. He's a slow mover, isn't he? My men didn't realize he belongs to you. They thought he'd cause a sensation in our circus. I was going to bring the animal back later today.'

The Parish Clerk produced the letter from the Minister of Health. The man agreed, 'Yes, of course, I realize we have no claim on Dino. But would you consider selling him to us?'

The Parish Clerk's voice rang out. 'No, we wouldn't dream of selling Dino. He's ours for good.'

Jed pressed his fingers into Dino's neck and whispered, 'Hear that?'

They started the slow journey back to the village. Jed walked in front of Dino, and Mr Holloway and the Parish Clerk followed in the car. Boys and girls kept pace with them while traffic queued up behind. Wherever Dino went a procession always seemed to form behind him. Mr Holloway leaned his head out of the car window.

'Turn left at the cross-roads, for goodness' sake, Jed,' he called out. 'Go down the old road.'

They soon left the town behind and the children regretfully turned back and went home. There was very little traffic on the minor road, which was just as well for Dino liked to stop now and then.

On one occasion they had a long wait while he slowly stripped all the leaves off a sapling. Then, just when they thought he was ready to go on again, he took it into his head to wander off the road, through a thicket, crushing young trees and shrubs as he went, and on to the adjoining railway line. As usual he left a stretch of crumpled fence behind him. He took no notice of the Parish Clerk's frenzied attempts to stop him as he ambled along the line.

'Oh, oh, more expense!' screamed the Clerk. 'The railway will make us pay for a new fence and also fine us for trespassing. Where's the money coming from? He'll have to – '

'Don't say it,' said Mr Holloway, exasperated. 'I'm tired of hearing you say, "He's got to go – He's staying – We can't afford to keep him – No one's going to take him away from us." You'll have to make up your mind about it. He belongs to us and he's staying. No matter what the cost.'

The Parish Clerk opened his mouth. 'Don't argue,' ordered Mr Holloway. He looked at his watch. 'Dino is on the Up line and it's half past eleven. The express will be along any minute. Jed, run along to the signal-box and alert the signalman. Quick as you can and we'll try to get Dino off the track.'

Jed raced along the top of the railway embankment as fast as his short legs would carry him. In spite of the efforts of the Parish Clerk and Mr Holloway, Dino loped along the line and, surprisingly, kept pace with Jed. He turned, gasping, and tried to wave Dino back, but still on he came. Jed climbed up the steps of the signal-box. The signalman was very surprised.

'A dinosaur – on the line? Blimey, I've had cows on the line, but never a dinosaur before.' He slammed levers hard over to reverse the signals to danger and then started back as Dino tried to push his head through the open window of the box.

'Goodness!' marvelled the signalman. 'There could have been a nasty accident, but I don't know who would have had the worst of it, Dino or the train!'

The train could now be seen in the distance and as it approached the 'home' signal, its brakes were rapidly applied and it screeched to a stand. The driver jumped down from his cab and came along the line. He stopped to examine something as he neared the signal-box.

Giving Dino a very surprised look, he called up to the signalman, 'What a mercy you were able to halt the train before it struck that telephone cable lying across the line.'

'What cable?' asked the signalman, mystified.

'Why, didn't you know about it? There, just in front of the train. I only missed it by a few inches. The police will have to get busy. I expect this is the work of mischievous boys. Pity they don't realize how many lives are at stake when they behave in this irresponsible manner.'

'I stopped the train because Dino was on the line,' explained the signalman.

Mr Holloway and the Parish Clerk came running up. 'Dino has done it again,' cried Jed. 'He's saved the express from being derailed.'

Passengers were leaning out of the windows all along the train. They had read about Dino in the newspapers and had seen the pictures of him on television, but to view a live dinosaur at such close quarters was something they wouldn't have missed for anything. Dino started to move forward, and for one awful moment Jed thought he was going to try and push the train back along the line, but he turned when Jed ran in front of him. Eventually they managed to get Dino through the thicket and back on to the road again. The passengers cheered and waved as the train drew away. The signalman called out.

'Don't concern yourselves about the damaged fence. We'll soon put that right.'

'Clever Dino,' laughed the Parish Clerk.

'"We wouldn't part with him for anything!"' said Mr Holloway, with a sidelong glance at Jed.

'No, no, of course not,' agreed the Parish Clerk innocently. 'I noticed yesterday Dino ate some bread put out for him. I think I'll order a dozen loaves a day for him. We must pamper him a little. He's so helpful!'

'Who's going to pay the baker for the bread?' asked Mr Holloway.

'Oh, really, what a silly question,' replied the Clerk.

As they neared the village, Dino insisted on turning down the lane leading to the old chalk-pit. He walked in a leisurely manner into the quarry and stood for a time looking down intently into the hole. They led him away, but as they were going back up the lane, they heard a crash behind them.

They turned and rushed back. Dino followed them. Hard on their heels came the workmen from the building site. They all gazed down into the hole which had appeared alongside the one already there. There was an awed silence, then,

'Do you see what I think I see?' whispered one of the men.

Mr Holloway knelt down and looked into the hole. He said solemnly, 'I should say there's another dinosaur down there!'

The Parish Clerk couldn't believe it. '*Another?* Another dinosaur?' he wailed. 'Just when I'd become reconciled to owning one dinosaur, but two . . .' He spread out his hands in despair. 'Two of that *size*, I ask you . . .'

'It will mean twice as much interest in our village,' smiled Mr Holloway.

'And twice as much expense,' moaned the Clerk. 'I won't be able to stand it. He'll have to –'

'Oh, no, no, no, he won't have to go,' put in Mr Holloway quickly. 'It has already been decided that Dino belongs to us, so I don't see how we can get out of adopting his twin as well, even if we wanted to, do you?'

'Go and get the cranes,' ordered the foreman. 'We're becoming used to this,' he added in a resigned tone of voice.

Jed, tense with excitement, watched the new arrival being hoisted out of the hole. This dinosaur was smaller than Dino. Had Dino grown with all the food and milk he'd been having, wondered Jed. Or was this a younger animal?

Jed whispered to Dino, who had his head well down, 'Hasn't it been a wonderful day? We've been told officially that you belong to us. And now you've got a playmate.'

Jed helped to gather wood to make a bonfire and soon the newcomer woke up and rose to his feet, just as Dino had done not so long before. News had spread round the village and a crowd soon gathered. People laughed and shouted as Dino's twin reared his head on the long, long neck and looked down at them.

'Well, Jed, what shall we call this one?' asked Mr Holloway.

'"Sauro", sir,' said Jed promptly.

'Sauro?'

'Yes. *Dino* . . . and . . . *Saur* – o.'

'Ha, ha, what do you think of that for a

79

name, Mr Parish Clerk?' asked Mr Holloway. But the Parish Clerk, poor man, was in
too much of a daze to understand properly
what was being said to him.

'Two,' he kept repeating to himself. 'I was
just about getting used to managing one, but
two dinosaurs . . . This village will never be
the same again!'